THE GHOST TOWER

THE GHOST TOWER

Gillian Cross

ILLUSTRATED BY
Sarah Horne

Barrington Stoke

First published in 2019 in Great Britain by
Barrington Stoke Ltd
18 Walker Street, Edinburgh, EH3 7LP

www.barringtonstoke.co.uk

A CIP catalogue record for this book is available
from the British Library upon request

ISBN: 978-1-78112-837-4

Printed in China by Leo

Contents

CHAPTER 1

The Tower on the Hill

Ryan and Dot lived next door to each other, on the edge of the village. At the very end of the road. There was nothing beyond their houses except a green hill with a steep stony path running up to the top.

Right up to the Ghost Tower.

The Ghost Tower was tall and dark, with stone walls that were covered in ivy. Ryan was used to it, because he had lived in the village all his life. But when Dot moved in next door, she

1

saw the tower for the first time – and she was very excited.

"It's like something out of a story!" she said. "There could be anything in there! A box full of gold! Or monsters! Or a hideout for spies! I have to see inside."

"No chance," said Ryan. "There's no way in. The door's blocked up and there aren't any windows except those big ones at the top."

Dot looked up at the windows and frowned. They were square holes, without any glass, right at the top of the tower. Much too high to reach, even with a ladder.

"So what is the tower?" she said.

"It's called the Ghost Tower," said Ryan.

"The *Ghost* Tower?" Dot's eyes glittered with excitement. "Why? Is it haunted?"

Ryan shrugged. "I don't know," he said. "That's just its name. It doesn't mean anything."

"It must mean something," said Dot. "Let's go and ask your mum."

But Ryan's mum didn't know either. "People have always called it the Ghost Tower," she said. "I don't know why. Maybe someone saw some ghosts up there."

Dot gasped. "Real ghosts?" she said.

Dot didn't say anything else about it. Not for a while. But every morning, as she and Ryan walked to school, she stared up at the Ghost Tower. The school was in the middle of the village, and Ryan and Dot always went together, but they didn't talk much. Dot just kept looking up at the tower. Chewing her lip, as if she was thinking hard.

Then one morning she said, "I've got an idea! Let's go up there. In the dark."

Ryan blinked. "Go up where?"

"To the tower, stupid." Dot's eyes were very bright. "Let's go up there in the dark and look for ghosts. Let's do it tonight! It would be brilliant if we saw a real ghost!"

Ryan went pale. "Would it?" he said.

"Of course it would!" Dot grinned. "I'll meet you at the bottom of the path. At eight o'clock tonight. OK?"

"Um ..." Ryan didn't know what to say. He didn't like the idea. But he didn't want Dot to think he was afraid.

Because she wasn't afraid of anything. She dived straight into the deep end of the swimming pool. She pushed into the big boys' football game – and scored three goals. She even loved the climbing wall in the school hall. Just looking at that wall made Ryan feel dizzy, but Dot climbed right to the top the first time she tried.

"Well?" Dot said. "Come on. Make your mind up. Are you coming or not?"

"OK," muttered Ryan. "I'll meet you at eight o'clock tonight."

CHAPTER 2

Out in the Dark

At eight o'clock that evening, it was very dark. Ryan's mum didn't want him to go outside.

"You won't be able to see," she said. "You might trip over something."

But his dad laughed. "Ryan's not a baby," he said. "He'll be fine if he takes a torch."

Dad found the big black torch in the kitchen and Ryan took it and went out to meet Dot.

She was already waiting, hopping around at the bottom of the path and keen to get going. When she saw the torch, she sniffed. "We don't want that! The light will scare the ghosts away."

"We need it for going up the path," Ryan said. "I'll turn it off when we get to the top of the hill."

Dot pulled a face but she didn't argue. They started to climb the hill together. The path was very steep, so they didn't talk until they were near the top. When they saw the Ghost Tower ahead, Dot looked at Ryan.

"Torch – off!" she whispered.

Ryan pressed the switch and the light disappeared. For a moment, they couldn't see anything at all. Then their eyes got used to the darkness. The Ghost Tower loomed in front of them like a giant black shadow.

"Ssh," whispered Dot. "No talking."

They crept forward towards the tower.
Their feet didn't make any sound on the
short soft grass and they didn't say a word.
Everything was very, very quiet.

Then suddenly, out of the Ghost Tower, a
great white shape swooped towards them.

It was totally silent, and it came without
any warning, zooming straight at them. Ryan
felt a rush of cold air as it went past his face.
He didn't think. He just turned round and
started running.

Dot was close behind him. They charged
back down the hill together. They were almost
at the bottom before Ryan remembered he still
had his torch. He turned it on and they stopped
to catch their breath.

"Wow!" panted Dot. "Oh WOW! We did it,
Ryan! We saw a real live ghost!"

But Ryan was thinking now. About the white shape that had come towards them. And the silent way it had flown. "I'm not sure ..." he said. And stopped.

"What?" said Dot.

"I don't think it was a ghost," Ryan muttered.

"Of course it was a ghost!" Dot said. "What else could it have been?"

"I think ... maybe ..." Ryan looked down at his feet. "I think it was a barn owl."

"A barn owl?" Dot scowled. "That's rubbish. If it was just a bird, why did you run away? Of course it wasn't a barn owl. It was a GHOST." She stomped off down the path without waiting for Ryan. He heard her open the front door of her house and slam it behind her.

He walked down the hill very slowly. He didn't want to quarrel with Dot, but he knew he was right. The white shape they'd seen was a barn owl. Not a ghost.

CHAPTER 3

The End of the Ghost Tower?

Dot didn't speak to Ryan for two days. She went to school without him and sat on the other side of the classroom. She didn't even look at him. She ignored him in their PE lesson too, when they were on the climbing wall. He was halfway up the wall and she went straight past him. He hadn't heard her coming and he was so surprised when she pushed past that his foot slipped and he nearly fell off.

It felt as if she was never going to speak to him again. But on the third day, she banged on his front door while he was having breakfast.

"Hurry up, Ryan!" she called through the letterbox. "I need to talk to you!"

Ryan's dad grinned. "Sounds as if she's in a hurry," he said. "Something important?"

Ryan shook his head. "No idea," he said.

"Well, you'd better go and see," said his mum. "Before she breaks the door knocker."

Ryan gulped down his last bite of toast and stood up. "Coming!" he called.

Dot started talking as soon as he opened the front door. "I've found out something terrible! About the Ghost Tower! My brother's just told me."

Dot's brother was grown up and he worked for the council.

"Told you what?" Ryan said.

"Some big company has bought the land over there." Dot waved her hand at the fields. "And they've bought the hill too. They want to build lots of houses – and they're going to knock down the Ghost Tower!"

"What?" Ryan couldn't believe it.

"It's true!" Dot said. "They say the tower is dangerous, so they're going to knock it down."

Ryan looked up at the hill. What would it look like without the Ghost Tower?

"We can't let them do it!" Dot said angrily. "We have to save the tower!"

"How can we do that?" said Ryan. "They're a big company and we're just a couple of kids. And they're right about the tower. It IS dangerous. That's why the door's blocked up. The staircase is rotten."

"Then they should mend it!" Dot said. "We can't let them pull the tower down. I want to see what's inside."

Ryan shook his head. "That's impossible. My dad says no one's been inside for fifty years."

"I don't care!" Dot said. "I'm going in. There has to be a way!"

She didn't say anything else all the way to school. She just frowned and stared at the ground. Ryan could see she was thinking very hard.

She didn't talk at break-time either. Just sat in a corner of the playground, staring up at the tower and chewing her bottom lip. She was very quiet all day. Until she and Ryan were walking home from school.

Then – when they'd said goodbye to all their friends and they were on their own – she said, "I've got an idea."

Another idea? Ryan looked at her. "What is it?" he said. He wasn't sure he liked Dot's ideas.

Dot opened her mouth. And then shut it again.

"What?" said Ryan. "What were you going to say?"

Dot stared at him. "It's a secret. Promise you won't tell anyone?"

"Is it about getting inside the Ghost Tower?" Ryan said. He looked at Dot's face. "It is, isn't it?"

"It might not work," said Dot. "And it could be … dangerous. But I have to try – before it's too late. Will you help me?"

Ryan didn't want to say yes. But if he didn't help, he knew Dot would do it anyway. What if she did something really dangerous? What if she got hurt? Then it would be his fault that he hadn't helped. "All right," he said slowly. "But only if we're careful."

"We'll be super-careful," Dot said. "Don't worry. I've worked it all out. We need to go to the tower in the dark, like we did before. But we'll be up there much longer. And we don't want people asking questions or finding out why we're out so late."

Ryan thought about it. "We could go on Tuesday," he said. "That's Hallowe'en. All the kids in the village go trick or treating, so no one will be surprised that we're out in the dark."

Dot grinned. "That's brilliant! And we can dress up as ghosts! If we wear sheets – really big ones – we'll have lots of room to hide things underneath."

"What kind of things?" Ryan asked. He was starting to feel nervous.

Dot gave a mysterious grin. "Things like … a ball of string. And some climbing ropes and helmets. I'll borrow those from school. And there's something else I have to borrow too. From my brother Ted …" She leaned closer to Ryan and started whispering in his ear.

*

Would Dot's plan really work? Ryan didn't know, but that night he was almost too excited to sleep. He opened his curtains and stared out at the Ghost Tower. It looked very black with the full moon behind it. He could see the stars through the big square windows at the top.

They were very high up …

And was there something moving up there? He peered at the windows. Could he see something fluttering, very faintly, in the darkness ...?

He was still looking when he fell asleep.

CHAPTER 4

Fat Ghosts

"Why do you want to be a ghost?" Ryan's dad said on Saturday. "You've got a fantastic skeleton suit. Wear that."

"But I'm going with Dot," Ryan said. "We're both going to be ghosts. FAT ghosts."

"Weird!" said Dad.

Ryan's mum put a hand on his arm. "Let them be ghosts if they want to. He can have one of our old sheets."

She found the sheet and Ryan spent the rest of the day working out where to cut the eye holes. He drew a round black mouth too, and made sure he could tie the sheet on firmly. It mustn't fall off!

Ryan made sure his phone was charged up as well. Just in case. He thought he might see the barn owl again and he wanted to get a photo this time.

*

On Tuesday evening, he went round to Dot's house as soon as it was dark. She opened the door and he crept in.

"Come into the garden," she whispered. "I've put all the things in the shed."

Dot had hidden everything she'd borrowed behind a pile of flower pots. There was a blue climbing rope, looped into a tight bundle. A ball of string. Two climbing helmets and two harnesses. And something else as well.

The small black drone Dot had borrowed from her brother Ted.

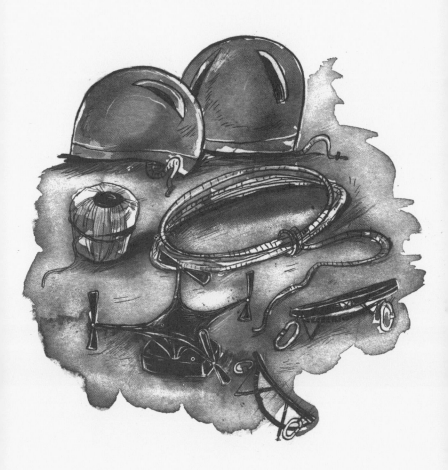

Ryan had seen Dot fly the drone lots of times and he knew she was good at it. But there was a lot of other stuff too. Could they hide it all under their sheets?

He began to feel nervous. Would Dot's plan really work?

"Scared?" said Dot.

"No!" Ryan said. Then he looked down at the climbing rope. "Well, a bit."

Dot grinned. "Don't worry. I've worked it all out. Let's go."

They put the harnesses on, under their ghost sheets, and clipped the helmets on to the front of the harnesses. That made them look like fat ghosts. Then Dot put the string and the climbing rope into a plastic bag.

"You take this bag," she said. "I'll take the drone."

The sheets hid everything, but by the time they were ready and it was all tied to their harnesses, they looked like VERY fat ghosts.

"Everyone's going to laugh at us," Ryan said.

"Good!" Dot grinned. "Then they'll give us lots of treats. Come on, let's go!"

They waddled out of the shed and back through Dot's house. When her brother saw them, he burst out laughing. "You won't scare anyone," he said.

"Woo-oo!" Dot grinned back at him. "We're FAT ghosts – because we EAT people!"

"Yum yum!" Ryan licked his lips.

Dot's mum was laughing. "Have fun!" she said. "Don't be too late. You have to be at school in the morning."

*

For a quarter of an hour, they walked through the village and knocked on people's doors. Everyone laughed and gave them chocolate and apples. When their pockets were full, they crept back to the bottom of the steep stony path.

Dot looked round to make sure no one was watching. Then she pointed at the bushes beside the path. "Quick! Hide your sheet in there," she said.

They took the sheets off and bundled them into the bushes. Then they started to climb the hill. It was very dark and they had to make sure they didn't lose the path. They couldn't risk using a torch this time.

When they got to the top of the hill, the tower looked very dark – and very, VERY tall.

"Quick!" whispered Dot. "Go round to the back!"

As they ran behind the tower, Ryan looked up at it. Maybe there really were ghosts inside. And even if there weren't, the tower looked very scary. It made him shiver, but he followed Dot round to the back. Because they had to carry out their plan. There would never be another chance.

Soon the tower would be gone.

CHAPTER 5

Up the Tower

Dot untied the drone from her harness. "Now I need the string," she said.

Ryan took the ball of string out of the bag and gave it to her. She tied the end of the string to the drone. Then she picked up the remote control. "Here we go," she said. "Hope I can do it."

She turned it on and away went the drone up the side of the tower, pulling the string behind it. Dot dropped the ball of string on the ground and they watched it unroll. Soon, the drone was high in the air, beside one of the tower windows, with a long trail of string hanging down behind it.

Dot let the drone hover for a moment longer. "This is the hard bit," she whispered. Carefully, she steered the drone through one of the big, square, empty windows, into the tower.

Ryan was watching – and he gasped. "Dot! Look!"

Just for a second, there was something else in the window space. A tiny dark shape fluttering above the drone.

Dot didn't take any notice. She was too busy thinking about the drone. Now it was inside the tower, they could hear it buzzing, but she couldn't see it. She had to guess how to steer it out of the next window.

Suppose she can't get it out? Ryan thought. *Suppose it gets stuck in there?*

But it didn't. After a couple of seconds, the drone flew out again, through the other window. Still pulling the string behind it.

Dot steered the drone back down to the ground. Then she grabbed it, turned it off and untied the string, which she held on to very tightly.

"Got it!" she said. She waved the end of the string at Ryan. "Now I need to tie this to the climbing rope."

She tied the string into a strong, careful knot around the end of the climbing rope. Then she nodded to Ryan. "OK. Now YOU wind up the string."

Ryan bent down and picked up the ball of string. Very slowly and carefully, he started to wind the ball up again. As he pulled, the long trail of string came back down the tower wall.

And up went the knot where the string
was tied to the climbing rope. Dragging the
climbing rope with it. Up and up. Back through
one window and out of the other. Then back
down the tower and into Ryan's hands.

Now Ryan was holding the knot that Dot
had tied. The rope went all the way up the
tower, in through one window, out of the other
and back down again, and the string was all
wound up into its ball again.

Dot undid the knot. She attached the rope to her climbing harness, the way they'd been taught at school. Then she put on her helmet.

"See what I'm doing?" she said to Ryan. "Once I'm up in the tower, you do the same thing. And don't forget your helmet."

She started climbing. She found holes to put her feet into, and bricks that stuck out where she could hang on with her hands. Ryan felt his heart thumping. *I can't do that*, he thought.

But he had to, if he wanted to get inside the tower. And there wasn't going to be another chance. If he didn't get inside the tower now, how would he feel when it was knocked down?

When Dot reached the window, she pulled herself into the tower and unclipped the ropes from her harness. Then she waved to Ryan, telling him it was his turn.

Now or never!

Ryan put on his helmet and attached the rope to his harness. He grabbed a lump of stone sticking out of the wall and felt around for a foothold.

Then he pulled himself up and felt around with the other foot.

Very slowly, he worked his way up the tower. There was no time to be afraid. All he could think about was finding another place for his hand. Then his foot. Then his other hand ...

Up and up and up ...

At long last, he felt the stone window ledge above him. He hauled himself up, until he was lying across it—

And then something flapped past him – and it wasn't the barn owl! It was something dark and fluttery and WEIRD.

A ghost!

Ryan gasped and slipped backwards, off the window ledge.

CHAPTER 6

Inside the Tower

For one terrifying second, Ryan thought he was going to fall all the way to the ground. Then the clip on his harness locked tightly on to the rope. He was safe, but he was dangling in mid-air.

Dot leaned out of the window and grabbed his arms. "It's OK," she hissed. "Keep climbing. Find a foothold."

At last, Ryan found a place for one foot. Then the other. Then Dot guided him onto the window ledge again. Somehow, he pulled himself up through the window, into the tower. There was a dusty wooden floor at the top of the tower. Ryan sat against the wall and got his breath back.

They were in a cold bare room with some rickety wooden stairs going down in one corner. The moonlight threw black shadows across the floor.

"There *is* a ghost," Ryan said. "It went right past me."

Dot hesitated. "I'm not sure it was a ghost," she said. "It was flying. And it came from up there, near the roof."

"Let's have a look." Ryan took out his phone and turned on the light.

He shone it up at the roof. There were lots of big wooden beams up there, high over their heads. And in between the beams were lots of small dark shapes hanging down. They looked a bit like bunches of dry leaves, no bigger than Ryan's hand.

But they weren't leaves. They moved. When the light shone on them, they twitched away from it, turning sideways. Ryan saw tiny pink faces.

"I think they're bats," he said.

"Bats?" Dot gasped. "Let's get out of here – before they start sucking our blood!"

"I don't think they're vampire bats," Ryan said.

"They're in the Ghost Tower!" Dot screeched. "Of course they're vampire bats!"

"But—" Ryan wanted to stay and have a better look at the bats, but Dot was pulling his arm, trying to drag him back to the window.

He took a couple of photos of the bats, as quickly as he could, zooming in to get close-ups. He could see the bats didn't like the flash. They kept twitching and turning away from the light. As he took the last picture, they suddenly started moving.

They came flying down from the rafters, right past Ryan and Dot. In a dark fluttering cloud, they streamed through the window, disappearing into the night sky. For a moment, Ryan couldn't breathe.

"Wow!" said Dot. "Oh, WOW!"

Ryan nodded. "That was ... amazing."

He wanted to stay and wait for the bats to come back, but Dot tugged at his sleeve. "We have to go!" she said. "It's getting really late."

She checked their harnesses and Ryan lowered himself out of the window. As they climbed down the tower, he kept thinking about

the bats. It had been a shock when they started flying, but they were beautiful.

"I wonder what kind of bats they are," he said as he and Dot walked back down the path.

"I told you," Dot said. "They're vampire bats." She shivered. "I wonder what they'll do when the tower is knocked down."

Ryan hadn't thought of that. *Maybe I'll look that up*, he said to himself. *What do bats do if they lose their home?*

CHAPTER 7

Very Special Bats

There was no time to look up anything that night. By the time they got home, it was almost ten o'clock and Ryan was in trouble. His mum dragged him into the house and sent him straight to bed.

"Go to sleep this minute!" she said. "Or you'll never get up in time for school!"

Ryan dreamed about the bats all night. But they weren't cruel and scary – they were little furry things with funny lumpy noses and big pointed ears. He kept wanting to stroke them.

Next morning, he sent Dot the pictures he'd taken. All day, she kept creeping up behind him and whispering, "Woo-oo! Vampire bats! Ready to suck your blood!"

Ryan was sure that wasn't right. The moment he got home from school, he turned on the computer and started searching for "vampire bats". And it didn't take him long to prove that Dot was wrong.

Totally wrong.

For a start, vampire bats weren't terrifying. They mostly sucked blood from cattle and horses, not people. And anyway, they lived in Mexico and South America. So the bats in the tower had to be something completely different.

Ryan did another search. And he found some very interesting pictures. He sent them to Dot. Then he sat back in his chair and waited.

He didn't have to wait long. A couple of minutes later, Dot was banging on his front door. And she was very, very excited. When he let her in, she waved her phone in his face.

"Are you serious?" she said. "Are you telling me those bats in the Ghost Tower are really ..." She peered down at the phone to check the name on the pictures he'd sent her. "Great-er horse-shoe bats?"

Ryan nodded. "Look at the pictures. Same pale-brown fur. Same funny lumpy noses. They've got to be greater horseshoe bats!"

"And they're really special?" Dot said.

"Seems like it." Ryan waved a hand at his computer screen. "I've looked them up on lots of different websites. They're really rare!"

Dot waved her arms and jumped in the air. "Don't you see what that means?" she cried. "We can save the Ghost Tower! If there are

45

rare bats inside, the company won't be allowed to knock it down! The council will stop them. I'm going to show Ted these pictures as soon as he gets back from work!"

Why Ted? For a moment, Ryan didn't understand. Then he remembered. Of course! Dot's brother Ted worked in the council offices. He was the perfect person to help them!

*

When Ted came back from work, Ryan and Dot were waiting for him. As soon as he opened the front door, Dot waved her phone in his face to show him the bat photos.

"Look at these pictures, Ted!" she said. "This one's from the internet. And the other one is from inside the Ghost Tower. See? They're the same! There are greater horseshoe bats inside the tower. And they're really rare!"

Ted took the phone and looked at the photos. "How did you get a picture from inside the tower?" he said.

Ryan's heart thumped. Now there was going to be trouble.

But Dot had an answer ready. "We used your drone," she said.

Which was true. In a way.

Ted stared at the pictures. "They do look the same," he said. "And if there are any bats in the tower it can't be knocked down. I'd better show these to my boss tomorrow morning."

"Yay!" said Dot. "We've done it! We've saved the Ghost Tower!"

But she spoke too soon ...

CHAPTER 8

Too Late

When Ted came back from work the next day, Ryan and Dot were waiting for him again.

"What happened?" said Dot. "Is the Ghost Tower safe now?"

Ted shook his head sadly. "Sorry. My boss says it's too late. They're going to knock it down on Monday."

"But what about the bats?" Ryan said.

"The company had a survey done last year," said Ted. "They didn't find any bats in the tower, so the council said it was fine to knock it down."

"But there ARE bats!" Dot said angrily. "Look at the picture!"

"Can you prove that picture was taken inside the Ghost Tower?" said Ted. "It could be from anywhere. My boss thinks it's just a trick."

"It's NOT a trick!" Dot stamped her foot. "The bats are there – we saw them! There must be something we can do to save them. Come on, Ryan – think!"

Ted shrugged. "I think it's too late. What can a couple of kids like you do against a big company?"

That was when Ryan had his Big Idea.

"We could have a Save the Bats Day," he said.

For a second, Dot stared at him, as if she didn't understand. Then her eyes lit up. "Yes!" she said. "We can have a march through the village on Saturday. And get people to dress up as bats. Or ghosts."

Ted nodded slowly. "That might get the march in the papers. But you need to tell everyone in the village. And get them to join in."

"How can we do that?" Ryan said. "There's not much time."

"We need to call a village meeting," said Ted. "In the school hall."

"Ryan and I can make posters! So everyone knows." Dot jumped up. "Come on, Ryan! Let's go and get started!"

The next day, the whole village was covered in posters that said:

Save the Ghost Tower!
Save our Bats!

Important Village Meeting
7 o'clock on Friday evening

There were posters in the school and in the shop. And tied to fences and lamp posts. And stuck up in the windows of people's houses. Wherever there was a space, Ryan and Dot put up a poster. And the posters worked! Some people were excited about the bats and other people wanted to save the Ghost Tower, but everyone in the village was talking about the meeting.

On Friday evening at seven o'clock, the school hall was full. Ryan and Dot had made a slide show about the Ghost Tower and the bats, and the meeting started with that. By the end of the slide show, people were even more excited. They couldn't wait to share their ideas.

"I've got lots of material people can use for fancy dress!" shouted Mrs Lane from the shop.

"And I'll phone the local bat group!" said Dot's mum. "They can bring their bat detectors and prove there are greater horseshoe bats in the tower!"

"We need to phone the local paper too—" said someone else.

"And the TV—"

"And put lots of stuff on social media—"

"I'll go home and set up a website!" said Mr Drew from the school. "And I'll start a crowd-funding appeal! If we get enough, maybe we can buy the Ghost Tower."

By the end of the meeting, there were lots of plans. Everyone hurried off to make phone calls and post on the internet and sort out their fancy dress, ready for the march on Saturday afternoon. Dot and Ryan walked back home together.

"I've got a great idea for something else we can do," Dot said. "But it has to be a surprise. Has your mum got any more old sheets?"

She started whispering in Ryan's ear as they went and slowly a smile spread across his face ...

CHAPTER 9

Save the Ghost Tower,
Save the Bats!

The next morning, Ryan and Dot got up very early, while it was still dark. They sneaked out of their houses and walked up the hill together, carrying a big plastic box between them. Dot had some string and a pair of scissors in her pocket.

When they reached the Ghost Tower, they emptied everything out of the box. Ryan's mum had given them five old white sheets. Ryan and

Dot turned the box upside down and took turns to stand on it.

Then they unrolled the sheets and reached up the walls of the tower as high as they could. They fixed the cloth to the ivy on the walls of the tower, making sure it was tied on firmly. They knew it would flap around in the wind. When all five pieces of cloth were fixed on, Dot and Ryan picked up the plastic box and hurried back down the hill as fast as they could.

When the sun rose, the village was in for a surprise ...

*

Ryan sneaked back into bed. An hour later, his mum came into his bedroom.

"Time to get up," she said. "We've got lots to do to get ready for the march." She walked across the room, pulled his curtains open – and gasped. "What's that?"

She stared up at the Ghost Tower as if she couldn't believe her eyes.

Yes! Ryan thought. He jumped out of bed and went to stand beside her. The tower looked even better than he expected. Five huge white ghost shapes were fluttering on the walls. The wind was blowing them around in a creepy, ghostly way, but it wasn't hiding their ghost-faces. They looked fantastic.

Ryan and Dot had painted those faces very carefully with thick black paint.

"Who did that?" Mum's eyes sparkled. "It's a ghost mystery!"

By the afternoon, there were ghosts inside their house too. As soon as lunch was over, Ryan and his mum and dad put on their ghost costumes. Mum and Ryan had sheets with faces painted on them, but Dad was a headless ghost. He had two tiny eye-holes in his sheet and a fake head made out of a football, to carry under his arm.

"Woo-oo-oo," he moaned in a ghostly voice as they left the house.

As they walked to the school, they met lots of other ghosts – and lots of bats too. Everyone in the village was dressed up. And they were all laughing and talking about the ghosts tied to the tower.

Dot was a bat with a lumpy pink nose and big spreading wings. When she saw Ryan, she waved her hand and made little squeaking noises. "Ee ee ee!"

"Woo-oo-oo!" said Ryan.

Even Mr Drew, who was the head of the school, was dressed up. He was a ghost, like Ryan and his mum, and he was sitting in the

school playground, handing out banners that said: SAVE THE BATS! and SAVE THE GHOST TOWER!

There was a reporter from the local paper with a notebook. She was busy talking to everyone and writing it all down. And there were two young men from the bat group, with a video camera.

"They're going to film the march!" said Dot. She was very excited. "And put it on the internet!"

*

It was a great march. They all walked round the village, shouting, "Save the bats!" and "Save the Ghost Tower!" Then they went up the hill and stood round the tower, holding up their banners. The ghosts that Dot and Ryan had tied on the tower were still there, flapping in the wind, and the young men from the bat group filmed everything. They were very excited.

"This is going to be a great video!" said one of them.

"We'll put it up on the internet tonight!" said the other. "With a link to the crowd-funding page your head teacher set up."

*

The video of the march went viral. In the first week, it was viewed ten thousand times. And people donated lots of money on the crowd-funding page.

"It's fantastic!" Ryan said. "My mum says we really might get enough to buy the Ghost Tower for the village."

But they didn't need to buy it. The big company couldn't knock it down after all, because of the bats. So they gave it to the village. And the village put all the crowd-funding money into a trust, to look after the tower and keep the bats safe.

"We did it," Ryan said when he heard the news. "We did it, Dot. We saved the tower. And everyone's saying this has made our village really special. They're saying—"

But Dot knew what he was going to tell her. She interrupted before he could finish the sentence. "They're saying we should have a Bat Festival. Every year!"

Ryan nodded. "Isn't that great? So everyone will dress up—"

"—as ghosts!" Dot shouted.

"And GREATER HORSESHOE BATS!" they yelled together.

And they did.

Fantastic Bat Facts

The bats that Ryan and Dot find in the Ghost Tower are a real species. Here are some more facts about them and other bats:

- There are over 1,300 species of bats in the world.

- Bats are more closely related to humans than they are to mice!

- Most bats eat insects. In tropical countries, they also eat foods like fruit, flowers, frogs, blood and sometimes even other bats.

- Bats can live for up to 30 years.

- The greater horseshoe bat is one of the largest species in the UK and the bats are about the size of a small pear.

- The bats are a greyish colour when they are young but change to a brownish colour as they get older.

- Sadly, the number of greater horseshoe bats in the UK has decreased by 90% over the last hundred years. We need to protect them!

(Based on information from the Bat Conservation Trust)

Our books are tested
for children and young people by
children and young people.

Thanks to everyone who consulted on
a manuscript for their time and effort in
helping us to make our books better
for our readers.